Adapted by Kimberly Morris

Based on the television series, "That's So Raven", created by Michael Poryes and Susan Sherman

Part One is based on the episode written by Michael Feldman

Part Two is based on the episode written by Maisha Closson

New York

Printed in the United States of America

First Edition
1 3 5 7 9 10 8 6 4 2

Library of Congress Control Number: 2005921764

ISBN 0-7868-4694-1

For more Disney Press fun, visit www.disneybooks.com
Visit DisneyChannel.com

Part One

Chapter One

Raven Baxter was a happy girl. She was wearing a killer outfit. Her two best friends, Chelsea Daniels and Eddie Thomas, were hangin' tight—left and right. Best of all, Devon Carter, the most gorgeous boy in San Francisco, stood less than six feet away. Life was good.

Chelsea nudged Raven with her elbow and looked sideways at Eddie. "Ooh, look, Rae. It's Devon Carter."

"Ooh, I know." Raven shot a quick glance at the divine Devon, trying not to make it obvious that she was totally crushing on him.

"So, how's it going with you two?" Eddie asked.

"Oh, great," Raven fibbed. "Things are really starting to happen between us."

Raven struck a flirty pose as Devon walked by. She struggled to keep her voice from sounding over-the-top thrilled to see him. "Hey, Devon."

"Hey, Rae." Devon gave her a shy smile, but he didn't stop to talk. He kept on walking and opened his locker on the other side of the hall.

Raven's best friends gave her a "you wish" look.

Okay. So he wasn't exactly falling down at her feet. But in Raven's world, the glass was always half full. "See?" she said to Chelsea and Eddie. "Before it was just 'Hey.' Now it's 'Hey, *Rae*.'"

Raven believed in being positive. She was *positive* Devon was the guy for her. That had to mean he felt the same way—or would.

Eddie and Chelsea exchanged a look that said, "Poor Raven, there she goes again. Grasping at straws."

For, like, two seconds, Raven wondered if maybe they were right. Maybe she was just kidding herself. Maybe Devon wasn't interested in her at all.

But then, she felt the noisy hall grow silent. Time seemed to stand still.

**Through her eye
The vision runs
Flash of future
Here it comes—**

I see Devon surrounded by a dreamy light. I see his face moving closer to mine. Closer . . . closer . . . closer . . .

Behind him I see . . . a giant teddy bear and a robot.

A GIANT TEDDY BEAR AND A ROBOT???
How weird is that?

Raven snapped back to the present. She'd just had a premonition that Devon was going to kiss her. Did it get any better than this? "Devon Carter is gonna kiss me!" she shrieked happily.

Some of the kids walking near Raven stopped in their tracks and stared at her as if she'd lost her mind.

Uh-oh! She was making a total fool of herself. "It's my favorite song," Raven added quickly. "*Devon Carter's gonna kiss me, gonna kiss me,*" she improvised, trying to make it sound like she was singing some hit tune.

But Chelsea knew exactly what Raven had said. She also knew her best friend was psychic. She clutched Raven's sleeve. "Wait,

Devon Carter is going to kiss you? When?"

"I don't know." Raven was so excited, she could hardly stand still. "But there was a robot and a giant teddy bear standing right behind him."

"What were they doing, lining up?" Eddie cracked.

"Ooh, Rae, you should ask him out," Chelsea urged. "I mean Devon Carter, not the teddy bear or the robot."

Raven suddenly felt shy. "Nuh-uh."

"Yeah," Chelsea insisted.

"No way."

"C'mon."

"Uh-uh. You think?" Raven asked.

Chelsea's raised eyebrows challenged her. "Yeah." Chelsea nodded, looking across the hall. Devon had just closed his locker and was heading off to class. It was now or never.

Raven took a deep breath and started

toward him. But then she chickened out. She whipped back around to face Chelsea. "You know, I was just thinking . . ."

She was stalling for time. But Chelsea and Eddie weren't going to let her get away with it. Together, they pushed her in Devon's direction. "Just go!" Eddie insisted.

Raven lurched toward Devon. He looked up and smiled. Luckily, she got her balance back before she fell right into him. "Oh, hey, Devon. Hey, hey," she babbled. "Hi, how you doin'?"

Devon smiled uncertainly and waited for her to get to the point.

"I was just wondering, if you're not doing anything this Friday, maybe you and me . . . I . . . you and I . . . We . . ." Raven lost her nerve and trailed off.

Devon finished the sentence for her. ". . . We could hang out?"

"Okay. I'd love to, thanks for asking," Raven said happily. Wow! she thought. The boy was smooth. He knew how to help a lady in distress.

"I'll call you," Devon said, ambling down the hallway.

Raven gave him a little wave. "Okay, I'll be waiting . . . by the phone, so patiently," she added in a small voice when he was out of earshot.

Raven hurried back to Chelsea and Eddie. What great buds. She would never have had the nerve to ask Devon out. All she'd needed was a little push. And they had given it to her. Literally.

"Okay, what'd he say, what'd he say?" Chelsea asked. "Tell me what he said."

"It's on for Friday. Just Devon and me . . . and a robot and a teddy bear. It's going to be so romantic!" Raven threw her arms open—

whap! whap!—accidentally smacking her friends and sending them sprawling.

After school, Raven did her best to beat her little brother, Cory, through the back door of the Baxters' house. Her master plan was to lock him out and hope he would run away and get lost.

Unfortunately, Cory poured on some last-minute speed and made it through the door, almost stepping on Raven's heels.

"Why do you always have to follow me?" Raven groaned as she put her books down on the kitchen counter.

"I was using your big head to block out the sun," Cory said.

Raven gave him a withering look. "Well, you know what? It was cute when you were born and when Mom and Dad brought you home from the hospital, but you're still here."

Cory's sour smile said, "You're so funny—not."

The phone rang. Raven immediately forgot about Cory and dove for the phone. It might be Chelsea. Better yet, it might be Devon.

But Cory's grubby little hand closed over the handset first. Before Raven could stop him, he was doing his pesky little-brother thing. "Baxter residence," he cooed in his pretend sweet voice. "Cute one speaking . . . Devon?"

Raven lunged for the phone, but Cory jumped out of reach. "Sorry, Raven's plucking her mustache right now."

Raven managed to grab Cory. "Give me that!" she snapped. She ripped the phone away, composed her face, and then spoke. "Hey, Devon."

Cory grabbed a bowl of grapes. Raven ignored him. She was not going to let her little gargoyle of a brother distract her while she made plans with Devon. Even the sound of his voice made her heart beat faster.

"Hey, Raven. The reason I called is, I can't hang out with you Friday night."

Raven's heart sank. Oh no! Cory began pelting her with grapes. Raven picked up a skillet from the counter and batted them away like tennis balls. "No! Why not?"

"I'm sorry, but I promised to take my little sister to Pizza Pals."

Cory threw another handful of grapes. Raven dodged them and tried to sound cool, calm, and collected. "Pizza Pals? What's Pizza Pals?"

"You know, the pizza place for kids," Devon explained. "They've got these crazy characters, like a robot and a giant teddy bear."

Cory ran around behind Raven. She could feel grapes bouncing off the back of her jacket. But who cared?

A robot and a teddy bear! Cory and his

grubby grapes disappeared. All Raven could see was the image in her vision. She remembered seeing Devon lean toward her—*with a robot and a teddy bear behind him*!

Fate! Fate! Fate! It was all adding up. Things were falling into place.

"I am so there!" Raven shrieked happily.

"What?" Devon asked.

Cory moved in for another grape attack. Raven reached out, grabbed the top of his head, and pulled him in close. Then she wrapped her arm around his neck and grabbed him in a headlock.

She looked down into his big brown eyes and thought, if you didn't really know Cory, you might actually think he was a nice little kid instead of a troll. "I mean, Devon, hey, you've got a little sister, and guess what? I have a little brother. So, you know, we could get them together."

Cory struggled, but Raven held on tight.

"Sounds cool," Devon said. "Because Nadine and I are really close. I think that's so important."

"So do I. In fact, my brother and I, we couldn't be much closer." She squashed Cory's face against her shoulder.

"Cool," said Devon.

"Yeah, so, anyway," Raven said, "we'll see you Friday night at Pizza Pals. Okay?"

"Later."

"All right. Bye, Devon." Raven disconnected the phone and allowed Cory to escape.

"No 'we' won't," Cory insisted, twisting away.

Raven spoke in a loving voice. "Cory, you know how Mom and Dad are always telling us that one day we're going to need each other?" Her eyes turned hard and determined. "That day is here," she announced.

"Then it's going to be a very expensive day for you," Cory warned, his brown eyes turning even harder and more determined than Raven's.

Chapter Two

Mr. Baxter was sitting next to Mrs. Baxter on the living room sofa. He put his arm around her and leaned in for a kiss. "Easy, tiger," Mrs. Baxter whispered. "The kids are still here."

Raven came down the stairs with Cory behind her. Mr. Baxter sighed. "What's taking them so long?"

"Cory doesn't do sweater-vests," Cory answered, hearing him from the stairs.

"Part of our deal was that I get to pick out your clothes," Raven said. "We have to be color coordinated, so Devon knows how close we are."

Victor Baxter turned to look at his children.

He wasn't exactly a fashionista, but even to him something looked wrong. Raven's outfit was okay. She was wearing some kind of lime green shirt with pants. But Cory had on a truly horrible pullover vest that was green-*ish*. In fact, it looked like one that had belonged to Mr. Baxter about forty-five pounds ago.

Cory tugged at the oversize V-neck vest. "I hate it."

Raven smiled determinedly. "No, you don't. You love it. Just like you love your loving sister."

Cory started to pull the vest off.

"Do you want me to kiss you again?" Raven threatened.

"No!" Cory cried in alarm. He pulled the vest back down.

Mr. and Mrs. Baxter both stifled their laughter. Mrs. Baxter jumped up to usher her children out. "Oh, look at our babies. All dressed up and heading for the door."

Mr. Baxter took his cue from her. Cory would survive being a fashion victim. The important thing was to get the kids out of the house so he and his wife could have a night to themselves. He opened the door and gave Cory a reassuring smile. "Yeah, I don't think I've ever seen you two look so cute. Go show the world."

Before Raven and Cory could even say good-bye, Mr. Baxter had closed the door firmly behind them.

Mr. Baxter gave his wife a meaningful look. "Alone, at last." He hurried to the CD player, pressed a few buttons, then swayed to the romantic music. "May I have this dance?" he asked Mrs. Baxter.

Mrs. Baxter smiled softly and took his hands. They danced together for a few moments, happy to have some time to themselves.

Ding-dong!

"I guess the kids must have forgot their key," Mrs. Baxter said.

Mr. Baxter groaned and headed for the front door. But when he opened it, it wasn't Raven and Cory. It was Chelsea and Eddie. And their arms were full of DVDs, board games, and grocery bags.

"Sorry, we forgot our key," Chelsea said. She and Eddie started into the living room. Mr. Baxter moved quickly to block their path.

But Eddie ducked under his arm. "Oh, that's my jam right there," he said, bobbing his head to the music. "Old school. C'mon, Mrs. B." He hurried across the living room floor and started to dance with Mrs. Baxter.

Mrs. Baxter reached over and turned off the music. "What are you guys doing here?"

Chelsea plopped her bags down on the sofa and dumped packages of pretzels, potato chips, cookies, and assorted junk food on the coffee table. "Hello? It's Friday night. We always hang here on Friday night."

"You know Raven's gone," Mr. Baxter reminded her.

Eddie shrugged. "Oh, that's cool. We like kickin' it here. You guys are the coolest parents."

Mr. Baxter couldn't help feeling flattered. "Really? Well, I guess we are 'da bomb.'"

Mrs. Baxter shot him a dirty look. "Well, we were until you said that."

Chelsea and Eddie plumped the couch pillows as if they were ready to settle in for a long visit.

Mr. Baxter began to get an uncomfortable feeling. Maybe being the coolest parents wasn't such a great thing after all.

When Raven and Cory walked into Pizza Pals, Cory shook his head. Whoa! He couldn't believe Raven was dragging him to this low-rent kiddie club. The place was full of old arcade games, dusty-looking stuffed animals, and a gazillion little kids and parents eating rubbery-looking pizza.

Then suddenly, Cory looked up and saw a huge set of grinning teeth. He and Raven both fell back a step.

The teeth belonged to a waitress in a red vest. "Hey, howdy-hello. I'm Randi. Welcome to Pizza Pals." Her canned greeting sounded like she'd already said it a thousand times that night.

Randi stuck pizza-shaped badges on Raven's and Cory's shoulders. "You're just in time for the show. Awesome!" She pivoted like a robot. Her bizarre forced grin never wavered.

"The show?" Raven looked at Cory. He shrugged.

Ta-da!

Raven and Cory jumped slightly as the restaurant vibrated with a tinny fanfare. Randi hurried away to greet some other guests, and the lights went down.

A recorded announcement boomed over the loudspeaker system. "Hey, kids, here comes Captain Pepperoni and his animatronic Pizza Pals!"

A spotlight illuminated a stage. The curtain went up, and out came the sorriest animatronic puppets Cory had ever seen. A giant teddy bear with a slide trombone. A stupid-looking robot with a drum. And a moth-eaten pirate with a banjo that looked like a pizza.

Raven clutched his arm. "Cory, Cory, it's them! The robot and the teddy bear! Omigosh, it's them." She jumped up and down, squealing.

Cory rolled his eyes. He couldn't believe Raven was so excited over these dumb puppets. "If you are a good little girl, you get to take your picture with them," he said in a sarcastic voice.

But Raven wasn't listening. She was entranced. The threesome rolled forward onto a little stage. They moved stiffly to the music, rotating left and right with their instruments.

"Pizza Pals, Pizza Pals.

Guys and gals love the Pizza Pals.

Order pies with extra cheese. . . ."

The announcer's voice broke in. "Two for ten dollars this week only."

"And the super big so-dees."

"Coupons not valid with any other offer," the announcer added.

"And you'll always be our favorite Pizza Pals!"

The pirate's jaw moved up and down, out of synch with the recorded voice. "See ya next show, mateys. Arrgggh!"

The characters rolled back into their alcove,

and the curtain came down. Kids and parents applauded. Cory wished they'd cut it out. He sure didn't want those puppets back for an encore.

But Raven actually looked disappointed that the show was over. She flagged Randi.

The grinning waitress hurried toward them with a jerky, perky gait. She looked like an animatronic character herself.

"Excuse me, miss," Raven asked her. "Where are they going? 'Cause I still gotta get my kiss from Devon."

"I have no idea what you are talking about," the grinning waitress chirped.

That makes two of us, thought Cory.

"But the Pizza Pals do a show every twenty-three minutes," Randi continued. "Every twenty-three stinkin' minutes," she muttered as she walked off.

Raven looked at her watch. "Every twenty-three stinkin' minutes," she repeated happily. Raven squirted breath spray into her mouth. She looked around nervously. Then her eyes lit up as a guy came into the restaurant carrying a little girl piggyback.

So that's Devon, Cory thought. Nice-looking dude. Cute little sister. She looked like a little doll with her corkscrew curls and frilly dress.

Raven ran over to them, and Cory followed.

Devon put the little girl down. "Hey!" he said to Raven.

"Hey, what's up, Devon?" Raven replied. She turned and gave the little girl a big smile.

"This is my little sister, Nadine," Devon said proudly.

Nadine cocked her head to the side and gave Raven an adoring smile. "Very pleased to meet you, Raven."

Cory watched Raven pretend to melt.

"Well, aren't you the cutest little thing? And this is my cuddly, adorable little brother, Cory. You guys are going to have hours of fun together."

Before anybody could say anything more, the grinning waitress was back. "Hey, howdy-hello. Looks like all my Pizza Pals are here. Awesome!" She pinned pizza badges on Devon and Nadine. "Follow me to the second-happiest place on earth."

"I want to walk with Raven," Nadine insisted.

Raven squeaked happily. This time, she looked like she really was going to melt. "She is *so* precious."

Nadine took Raven's hand and looked up at her adoringly. Cory guessed it was a girl thing. He hoped Raven wouldn't get a swelled head over it. She was already obnoxious enough.

Cory and Devon walked toward the table. Nadine and Raven walked behind.

Then all of a sudden, right behind him, Cory heard a big thump followed by a loud "OW!"

Chapter Three

Raven lay facedown on the floor, trying to figure out what had happened. She'd been walking beside Nadine. Then suddenly, she'd felt something between her ankles. A foot. A little bitty foot. A little bitty foot wearing little bitty sandals.

"Oh, Raven. I'm so, so sorry!" Nadine cried, pretending to be sincere.

Raven lifted her head and felt her face for damage. "That's okay. My chin broke the fall."

"Let me help you up." Nadine bent down. Her face appeared beside Raven's.

But sweet, little, precious Nadine wasn't looking so sweet or precious. In fact, little bitty Nadine's little bitty face was twisted into a hideous and frightening scowl. "Your nightmare is just beginning," she hissed in a soft voice that only Raven could hear.

"What?" Raven was stunned.

"Stay away from my brother," Nadine warned, helping Raven stand. In an instant, her scowl turned into a sweet smile, and she turned her face upward toward her brother. "Devy! Can I ride the horsey?" she begged sweetly.

Devon smiled, obviously under the impression that Nadine was the little princess she pretended to be. He helped her scramble up onto his back, and they galloped away.

Raven watched them, her mind spinning. Appearances were deceiving. Nadine looked like a sweet little girl. But she wasn't.

Well, two could play at this game, Raven thought. Cory looked like a sweet little boy. But he wasn't.

Thank goodness!

* * *

After a quick trip to the ladies' room to repair her damaged makeup, Raven found Cory playing a video game. She grabbed him by the collar and pulled him away.

"Hey, can't a man relax?" he complained.

"Cory, we had a deal," Raven said. "You're supposed to keep Nadine busy."

"She's doing fine." He pointed toward the other side of the arcade. Devon and Nadine were playing Gopher Smack. Each of them held a foam-rubber mallet. When little plastic gophers popped up out of their tabletop holes, Devon and Nadine smacked them with the mallets.

Devon caught Raven's eye and waved her over. "Hey, Rae. Check it out. This is fun."

Nadine waved her mallet. "Yeah, c'mon, Raven."

Raven thought about telling Cory to watch

her back. Then she figured, what the heck? There were people around. Devon was standing right there. What could Nadine do to her in front of so many witnesses? "Okeydokey."

Raven walked over to the Gopher Smack game. Nadine gave Raven a winning smile. Devon looked fondly at his little sister. It was clear he thought Nadine was making a great impression on Raven.

Nadine fluttered her eyelashes at Devon. "Devy, I need some more tokens." She indicated that he should leave and give her and Raven some time alone for "girl talk."

Devon winked. "Sure, Deeny." Devon handed Raven a soft-foam mallet. "Here." Then he hurried away.

Nadine smiled and held up her mallet. "Ready?" she asked Raven.

"For what?" Raven asked suspiciously.

Nadine giggled. "To play the game, silly."

She was so cute, Raven began to wonder if she'd imagined the whole tripping thing. Maybe she'd hit her head in the fall. Maybe it had just been a bizarre and ugly hallucination.

Nadine pressed the button. One after the other, little plastic gophers came popping up out of their holes.

Whack! Whack! Whack! Raven smacked the little gophers, and they dove back down. Okay, so it wasn't exactly chess. But it was still fun. There was something oddly satisfying about whacking a little plastic gopher with a foam-rubber mallet. Go figure!

Nadine circled around behind Raven—and smacked her mallet against the back of Raven's knees.

"YEOW!"

Raven's legs collapsed underneath her, and she went down.

Smack! Whack! Smack! Whack! Nadine pummeled her with the foam-rubber mallet. This wasn't Gopher Smack. This was Raven Smack. "Hey . . . hey . . . hey . . ." Raven protested.

But it was too late. Nadine was into it. Big-time. "My-brother-only-has-time-for-me!" she chanted, whacking harder and harder at Raven with her mallet.

"Ouch! Ouch!" This was horrible. Terrible. Raven's dream date was being ruined by a demonic little girl armed with a foam-rubber mallet.

Luckily, Devon appeared and Nadine immediately stopped. "I've got the tokens," he said. He noticed Raven cowering against the game table. "Raven, you okay?"

Raven rubbed her arm, wondering if she should blow the whistle on Nadine.

"She just had a little accident," Nadine told

Devon, her eyes daring Raven to contradict her.

"Yeah, then that mallet fell on me. Again and again and again—" Raven's eyes met Nadine's, but Nadine looked away and pointed. "Look, our pizza's ready!"

"Great, I'm starved," Devon said, and headed for their booth.

Raven started to follow him, but Nadine raised her mallet again and narrowed her eyes. Raven stepped back and let Nadine go first. Okay. Okay. The night was still young.

Nadine laughed nastily and ran after Devon.

Raven rubbed her arm and followed them toward the booth. "This kiss better be worth it," she muttered to herself.

On the way to the table, she saw her secret weapon with a cute girl around his own age.

"So," Cory asked her in a flirty voice, "what do you like on *your* pizza?"

Man! It was hard to keep the boy on task. Once again, Raven grabbed him by the collar. "Cory, get over here."

Cory tried to pull away, but Raven had him in a death grip. He made a "call me" sign to the girl and reluctantly fell into step beside Raven.

Devon and Nadine were waiting for them at the booth. Devon slipped in.

Nadine was just about to slide in beside him, but Raven managed to edge past her and get in first. "In your face, pipsqueak," she muttered, taking the spot beside Devon.

Squish!

"That didn't sound too good," said Raven. Then she felt something underneath her. What was it?

She slid quickly out of the booth. Oh no!

A big slice of pizza was stuck to her butt.

"Now it's in *your* face, grandma." Nadine snickered under her breath.

Cory laughed, too. What a traitor.

"Hey, Cory, what are you laughing at? This is your piece." Raven peeled the pizza off her rear and tossed it onto Cory's plate.

That shut him up.

Chapter Four

Meanwhile, back at Casa Baxter, Mr. Baxter sat on the floor next to Mrs. Baxter. He leaned against the coffee table with his elbow, reading the TEST YOUR NUTRITION IQ on the back of the Crackers 'n Sprouts box.

Trust Chelsea to bring eco–junk food. The quiz was boring. Still, it was more interesting than the movie.

Chelsea blew her nose with a loud honk as the hokey video came to an end. "You guys, this was like the third time I've seen *My Big Fat Monkey Wedding*, and every time it gets me."

Mr. Baxter ran a mental review of the evening's events. He wasn't quite sure how Chelsea and Eddie had managed it. But somehow he and his wife had wound up sitting on the floor while Chelsea and Eddie lounged on the couch. And somehow the Baxters had been sucked into watching that awful movie.

Thank goodness it was over. Maybe Chelsea and Eddie would go home now.

Chelsea blew her nose again.

"Get over it, Chels," Eddie urged. "Hey, it's time to play Contwingo."

Chelsea jumped up, excited. "Oh, you're right. I'll lay out the Contwingo mat and the Contwirler and the Contwimer."

Eddie pulled the coffee table aside so they would have more room. Unfortunately, Mr. Baxter's elbow was still on it.

"Yeow!" Mr. Baxter fell over.

Before he could protest, Chelsea produced a plastic mat with numbered footprints and hand-prints, a small hourglass timer, and a spinner.

Mr. Baxter managed to catch his wife's eye

as he climbed to his feet. She gave him a look of agreement. Enough was enough. It was time to invite their guests to leave.

"Oh, kids," Mrs. Baxter began, "it's getting late and—"

Eddie looked at her and began to cluck like a chicken.

Mr. Baxter's heart sank. Oh, no.

A deep line formed between Mrs. Baxter's brows, and her nostrils flared. "I know you didn't just cluck at me," she said slowly.

Chelsea smiled wickedly. "Oh, I'm sorry, I believe he just did."

"Baby, let it go," Mr. Baxter begged his wife. "It was just a cluck."

Tanya Baxter was a beautiful woman. A loving wife. A devoted mother. But she was also insanely and irrationally competitive. And everybody knew it—including Eddie and Chelsea.

"Not in my house," Mrs. Baxter declared. "Spin that Contwirler, girl!"

Mr. Baxter felt the rest of the evening going south. Once Mrs. Baxter's competitive spirit kicked in, she was relentless.

Chelsea spun the spinner. "Okay, right hand, nine. Left knee, seven."

Mr. Baxter felt Mrs. Baxter pushing him. "Go get 'em, tiger," she urged.

Sighing, Mr. Baxter stretched his left foot and his right hand.

CRUNCH!

Mr. Baxter froze. Was that his back? His hand left the mat. He grabbed his lower spine and braced himself for the pain he knew was coming.

Eddie giggled and held up an empty water bottle. He squeezed it and produced another awful crunch sound. "Gotcha, Mr. B! Psyched your mind."

Chelsea pointed to Mr. Baxter's hand, which was clutching his back. "Dude, you moved your hand. Two points for us." She and Eddie high-fived each other.

Mr. Baxter stepped off the mat. "They con-tricked me!"

Mrs. Baxter's mouth formed a grim line.

Mr. Baxter sighed. It was going to be a long night.

"Cory, how does it look?" Raven dipped some napkins in a pitcher of water and scrubbed hard at her rear.

There was still a perfect pizza-shaped stain on her pants. "Can't even tell," Cory lied.

Raven tossed the napkins into the trash. "Good. Now listen, man, you've got to start doing your job. Take this bucket of tokens. When I suggest that you and Nadine go play some games, you act excited. All right?"

"Got it," Cory said.

"Good." Raven hustled him through the restaurant and back to their booth. Devon and Nadine sat munching pizza. "Hey, everybody, I have an idea," Raven said in her most enthusiastic voice. "Cory, why don't you and Nadine go play some games?"

"Neh," Cory said, deliberately departing from the script.

Raven glared.

Heh! Heh! Heh! This was turning into a great evening. He got to watch Raven wipe out *and* ruin her outfit. Just when he thought it couldn't get any better, he was getting a chance to botch up her love life.

"Go on, Nadine," Devon urged. "You guys should get to know each other."

"Okay, Devy," Nadine said. She gave Devon a hug.

Cory's heart sank. Darn! Now he was actually going to have to spend time with Little Miss Muffet.

Raven gave Cory a gentle shove. "Take your time."

Cory reluctantly walked with Nadine to the Claw machine and dropped a token in. Nadine hovered at his elbow, watching. He ignored her and hoped she would buzz off.

The Claw machine was a huge plastic box, full of junky-looking toys—stuffed animals, balls, dolls. Players used levers to manipulate a huge claw inside the box. The object of the game was to snag a toy with the claw.

"I want that blue monkey," Nadine said.

Cory fiddled with the levers, fishing for a soccer ball. "Yeah? And I want a million bucks. Life is tough."

He turned to see if she was going to burst out crying or something. But what he saw in her face made him recoil. There was something menacing . . . something scary . . . something *evil* . . . in her eyes.

"I *said* . . . I want that blue monkey," Nadine repeated. Bad mojo rose off her like steam off a radiator.

Cory's heart began to hammer. He felt a cold sweat break out across his forehead. "Okay, then," he said hoarsely.

Raven slid a bit closer to Devon. "So, here we are," she said sweetly.

"Yeah," Devon said. "I'm really glad you came tonight, Raven."

"So am I," Raven agreed. "It's really nice that we can finally be alone."

"Just me and you." Devon looked deep into Raven's eyes.

Wow! This was definitely a romantic moment. But was it the moment? Raven looked over Devon's shoulder. The stage was dark. "No robot, no teddy bear," she murmured. "But hey, who needs them?" She leaned toward Devon, getting ready for her kiss.

Devon leaned toward her. Their lips were just about to meet when Nadine popped up from under the table, pushing them apart. "Cory won me a monkey!"

"Hey, Deeny!" Devon said.

"Hey, Deeny," Raven echoed, feeling venomous. She was going to kill that Cory. He was supposed to be keeping Nadine busy so Raven could collect her kiss. Where was he, anyway?

Hold it! Wait a minute. "Deeny, where's my brother?"

Nadine smiled innocently. "He really got into the game."

Raven jumped up. Nadine had done something awful. Raven just knew it. That's why the little girl looked so happy. Raven ran through the game arcade. Where was Cory? What had she done?

Just as she ran by the Claw machine, she saw something familiar pressed against the glass.

Cory's face!

He was inside the box of toys with his face pressed up against the wall.

"Cory! What are you doing in there?" Raven yelled. She could see his mouth moving, but she couldn't hear him. His lips formed the word "Help."

A little boy came running up to the Claw machine and grabbed the controls.

"Mommy! I want that big head," said the little boy, jerking the lever.

Cory's eyes widened as the wicked-looking claw moved toward him.

Raven pushed the little boy out of the way

and grabbed the controls. "I'll get you a duck, little boy. The big head's mine."

Raven was glad to know Cory was alive and well.

Because now she could kill him.

Chapter Five

Usually, Victor Baxter loved the feel of his wife's cheek pressed against his. Tonight, though, the cheek-to-cheek thing was not exactly working for him. He and Mrs. Baxter were twisted around each other, trying to beat Chelsea and Eddie at Contwingo. "Well, we're finally together," he said as his wife reached over him.

Eddie spun the Contwirler. "Okay, left ear, twenty-two, Mr. B."

Mr. Baxter tried to steady his balance. "Here goes." He stretched his head to put his ear down in box twenty-two.

CRUNCH!

"You're not gonna get me with that fake

water-bottle trick again," Mr. Baxter told Eddie.

Eddie looked worried. "I didn't do anything."

"Uh-oh! Here comes the pain," said Mr. Baxter, realizing he hadn't been tricked. He grabbed his back and collapsed. "Uggghhh!"

"Contwingo!" Eddie and Chelsea shouted victoriously.

"Rematch! Victor, get off your Contweester," Mrs. Baxter ordered.

Mr. Baxter groaned and shook his head. "I think we ought to call it a night."

Chelsea looked truly worried. "Wow, I'm really sorry about your back, Mr. B."

Eddie nodded. "Yeah. You should get some rest. . . ."

"Yeah," Mr. Baxter wheezed.

". . . so you're ready for next week," Eddie

finished with a broad grin. He pulled the mat out from underneath Mr. Baxter.

"Ow!" Mr. Baxter yelled.

Eddie and Chelsea quickly bundled up their games and gear and hurried out, closing the door behind them.

Mrs. Baxter put her hand on Mr. Baxter's arm. "I'm sorry I got carried away, baby. How's your back?"

Mr. Baxter smiled wickedly. "It's fine. I just faked it so we could have time alone." He reached behind him and produced another water bottle. He squeezed it to show how he'd produced the awful back-crunching sound.

"You did that, for us?" Mrs. Baxter gasped.

"Yeah." He waited for her to throw her arms around him and thank him. Instead, she gave him a dirty look and slapped his arm. "What's wrong with you? We could have won!" She ran to the door and called out to Chelsea and Eddie, "Get back here! It's not over!"

She clucked and flapped her arms like wings, taunting them.

Mr. Baxter groaned. Oh no! Here we go again!

It wasn't easy, but Raven finally managed to get Cory out of the Claw machine. She put one hand firmly against his back and steered him back to the table.

"Thanks for getting me out of the Claw." Cory was very subdued—for Cory.

Raven figured a near-death-by-Claw experience would calm almost anybody. So instead of killing him, she decided to be nice. "No problem. I still don't understand how Nadine got you in there."

Cory spun around, upset. "Raven, she can do things. Scary things. I want to go home."

"Cory, we can't go home, okay?" Raven said.

"I had a vision, and we can't leave until it comes true."

"Your vision, your problem," Cory replied as he started to walk away.

Raven caught his sleeve. "Cory, listen," she confided. "The vision I had was that Devon was going to kiss me during the Pizza Pals show."

Cory grimaced. "Ew, don't gross me out with your love life."

"I know you don't understand now, but I really, really like him, and this might be my only chance," Raven explained.

"Oh, I understand smoochin'," Cory said. "I just don't understand why somebody would want to smooch with you."

Raven stopped. Wow! What a mean thing to say. She felt her face fall.

"But if it's that important to you, I'll help out," Cory said quickly, clearly sorry that he'd been so nasty.

"Thanks, little brother. You're the best." Raven gave him a hug. A real hug, not a pretend one.

"I know," Cory joked. "You'll be getting my bill."

Together, they went back to the booth. Randi the grinning waitress hovered nearby, pasting badges on newcomers.

Raven looked at her watch. It had been twenty-two-point-five minutes since the last show. She wriggled happily in her seat. "All right, you guys. It's time for the big Pizza Pals show." She licked her lips to make sure her lipstick was in place.

Randi turned, overhearing. "Ooh, sorry, show's canceled."

Raven's mouth fell open. "No! It can't be canceled!" she cried.

"Sorry, but we're having some technical difficulties with our pirate," Randi explained.

"No!" Nadine whined. "Captain Pepperoni is my favorite."

"Mine, too!" Raven chased after Randi. "Wait, wait, wait," she said, starting to get desperate. "You don't understand, the show must go on. The robot, the teddy bear . . . Think of the children!"

"Okay, here's the deal," Randi chirped. "I'm really tired. I've worked a double shift, the pirate's leaking oil, *so back up off me*." Still grinning, Randi clenched her teeth and ground them.

Whoa! Randi was *this* close to snapping. Raven didn't want to be within arm's reach when she did. She quickly backed away.

"Awesome!" Randi did her robotic pivot thing and hurried away.

Raven felt like grinding her own teeth. "I did not put up with all of this to not get my kiss," she said to herself.

She hurried back to the table. Nadine put her head against Devon's shoulder. "Devy, I want to go home." Her voice was plaintive.

Devon gave her a reassuring hug. "Okay. I'm sorry, Raven, she was really looking forward to that show." He and Nadine started to get out of the booth.

Raven held up her hands. "No! Wait, wait, wait. The show is going to go on. Whatever it takes. I'm going to make sure they put the pep back into Captain Pepperoni. So, stay. Don't move."

Raven ran off. She'd come too far to give up now. In this bizarro world, nothing was as it appeared to be. Why should an animatronic pirate be any exception?

Cory sat in the booth with Devon and Nadine, wondering if Raven had lost her mind completely. From what he could see, this had to be the worst first date in the whole history of dating. Why couldn't they all just go home? Let everybody get out of their pullover vests and get on with their lives.

"This is so boring," Nadine complained. "If there's no show, I want to go home."

Devon gave her a pat. "Okay, Deeny. Just let me say good-bye to Raven first."

"Why? She probably already left," Nadine said. "She doesn't care about us."

Cory felt it was his duty to set the record straight on that one. "Oh, trust me. She cares."

Suddenly, the lights dimmed.

Ta-da! The electronic fanfare boomed. The crowd of cranky kids and parents cheered.

"Look, Deeny, the Pizza Pals' show *is* going on!" Devon exclaimed.

Nadine turned around so she could see the stage.

"Hey, kids!" bellowed the electronic

announcer. "It's time for Captain Pepperoni and his animatronic Pizza Pals!"

The curtain opened. The robot, the teddy bear, and the pirate rolled out on a platform. Cory noticed that the pirate seemed to wobble but then regained its balance. Maybe it was the oil-leak thing. He looked at the pirate closely, trying to see where he was leaking. Hey, wait a minute. . . . There was something very familiar about that pirate. Oh no! "Man, is she desperate," said Cory.

He watched Raven try to time her mouth and hand movements to the recorded song. He wondered where the real animatronic pirate was. Wherever he was, he was bald and naked. Raven had taken his wig, his beard, his hat, his clothes, and his banjo. She even had his eye patch!

"Pizza Pals, Pizza Pals.
Guys and gals love the Pizza Pals.

Order pies with extra cheese. . . ."

"Two for ten dollars this week only," boomed the announcer.

"And the super big so-dees."

"Coupons not valid with any other offer," the announcer reminded them.

"And you'll always be our favorite Pizza Pals!"

The animatronic characters began their fake, prerecorded jam session, swiveling left and right.

Cory watched Raven dodge the trombone and swivel away from the drum, while her hand moved up and down in a fake banjo strum. She moved her head left and right.

Dang! She was good! Better than the real Captain Pepperoni.

"There's something weird about Captain Pepperoni," Nadine complained.

"Oh, you have no idea," said Cory.

The music got louder and faster. Raven

ducked and swiveled and bobbed, dodging the trombone and the drum as they moved faster and faster.

Left . . . right . . . up . . . down. Raven's timing was perfect—until the teddy bear's slide trombone took her by surprise and knocked her hat off.

She ducked down to grab the hat, and when she came back up, the robot had swiveled around.

Raven's head popped up through the robot's drum, breaking the drum and jamming the gears.

But the band played on. The robot's arms went up and down, holding the drumsticks and drumming on Raven's head.

Raven boxed the robot a couple of rounds before managing to escape. She grabbed her banjo again—but the teddy bear's slide trombone snagged her beard.

Back. Forth. Back. Forth. The slide trombone tugged at the beard and shook Raven's head as if it were a rag doll's.

"Cory, what is going on up there?" Devon demanded. "That's *Raven*!"

"Rae didn't want you to leave because she really likes you," Cory said.

"Raven really likes me?" Devon said, surprised.

"Duh!" Cory and Nadine said in unison.

Devon smiled happily.

Cory couldn't believe Devon was so clueless. "Man, you got a lot to learn about the ladies," he told him.

Onstage, Raven was fighting for her life. The robot was drumming on her back, and the teddy bear was about to slide-trombone her to death. Smoke rose from underneath the stage.

Raven finally managed to free herself from

the trombone. As it came toward her again, she pushed it away with a shove.

The teddy bear swiveled completely around and . . .

Bang!

. . . smacked Raven on the back of the head.

Raven went flying forward, off the stage, and onto the floor.

Chapter Six

The music sputtered out, and the animatronic Pizza Pals ground to a stop.

Raven lay on the floor, feeling dizzy and slightly sick. She seemed to be spending a lot of time on this floor.

Then she opened her eyes and gasped.

There was Devon. He was leaning over her. She could see the robot and the teddy bear in the background. *It was just like her vision.*

"Raven," Devon said.

Raven curved her lips into a smile and waited. Here it came. Her kiss. Finally.

She waited.

"Are you okay?" he asked.

"Never better." She puckered slightly and closed her eyes.

"Good," Devon said. "Because you hit the deck pretty hard. I mean, what were you thinking, going up there?"

Raven opened her eyes. Come to think of it, in the vision he hadn't actually kissed her. He'd just leaned toward her—the way he was leaning now. She had assumed he was going to kiss her. But now she realized all he was doing was making sure she wasn't dead.

She sat up. She was totally embarrassed and disappointed. "Yeah, what was I thinking?" Devon probably thought she was a total nut case. An idiot.

"But I'm glad you're okay," he added. Then, he leaned in closer and pressed his lips against hers.

The kiss was a surprise—to both of them. Raven and Devon looked into each other's eyes. Devon suddenly seemed as unsure of himself as Raven. "Um, that was for being nice to my sister," he said in an embarrassed voice.

"You got any more sisters?" Raven asked eagerly.

Devon just grinned.

Cory and Nadine watched the little romantic drama from the booth. "Kind of makes you sick, doesn't it?" he said.

Nadine's shoulders slumped. "Don't get me started. We used to have fun until girls started to like Devon. Now I barely get to hang out with him."

"So," Cory asked in a conversational tone, "are you going to make Raven's life miserable every chance you get?"

Nadine slurped her soda. "That's the plan," she said in a businesslike tone.

Cory smiled. "It's going to be fun working with you," he said.

On Monday morning at school, Raven hurried toward Chelsea and Eddie. "Hey, y'all."

"She's still smilin'," Eddie said to Chelsea. "She must have had fun with Devon."

"Yeah, but was it worth missing Contwingo?" Chelsea asked.

Raven was still so thrilled and happy, she could hardly talk without squeaking. "It was awesome. We took our relationship to a whole new level."

Devon came around the corner. He looked incredible. He was so adorable. And Raven felt so close to him after all they had shared. "Oh, hey, Devon," she said happily.

Devon looked almost startled to see her. "Hey, Raven."

Raven waited for him to say something

personal. Something intimate. Something romantic. Something that would show Chelsea and Eddie how close they were.

Devon smiled shyly, then quickly looked down at his shoes.

Maybe he just needed a little time to compose his thoughts. Raven gave him an encouraging smile.

The awkward pause went on and on. Finally, Devon seemed to find the courage to speak. "Later," he said shyly. Then he hurried away.

Okay. So he still wasn't falling at her feet. But that glass was definitely still half full. "You see?" Raven said to Chelsea and Eddie.

It was clear from their faces that Chelsea and Eddie didn't.

But they would. They would. Raven was *positive*!

Part Two

Chapter One

Ticktock! Ticktock! Raven Baxter gazed into Devon Carter's gorgeous face, wishing he would hurry up and ask her out. The bell was going to ring any minute.

BRRINNNNGGGGGG!!!

The crowded school hallway emptied out fast. Students scattered in every direction to get to class.

Devon didn't even seem to hear the bell. He was gazing into Raven's eyes.

Raven heard it, but what the hey! If Devon was happy, no way was she going to break eye contact. So what if she was late for class. It was a small price to pay for love.

"Anyway," Devon said, as if he had all

the time in the world. "I was thinking . . . if you're not doing anything this weekend, I've got two tickets to the Blue Rain concert."

"Blue Rain! That's amazing!" Raven's breath left her lungs with a big whoosh. Her mind whirled like a pinwheel. *A date! A date! A real date!*

"So you like them?" Devon asked.

"Never heard of them," she squeaked. Oops! That was *not* what she meant to say. But she was too happy and excited to care.

"They're this really cool band," Devon said. "Everyone paints their face blue for the show."

Raven smiled seductively and pointed to her face—which she had carefully made up to look especially gorgeous. "I gotta paint this?" she teased.

"Don't worry. You'll look great. I gotta get to class." Devon ambled away, and Raven sighed, watching him. Devon was fantastic. And she and Devon together were . . .

. . . *really* late for class.

"Oh, snap!" she yelled, breaking into a run.

Eddie Thomas looked nervously at the clock. Where was Raven? Mr. Halloway hated it when students were late to his science class. And Raven was starting to make a habit of it.

Mr. Halloway stood in front of the class in his white lab coat and surveyed the room. "Remember, your science projects are due Friday. And please, people, a little originality. No papier-mâché volcanoes. If I see one more of those things, I may erupt myself."

The class laughed but broke off when Raven burst into the classroom.

Uh-oh! Eddie had a feeling Raven was about to meet up with a big-time eruption from Mr. Halloway.

Raven saw Mr. Halloway's face and read it correctly. She turned her head and shouted into the hallway. "You take care of that snakebite, Timmy." She rapped her fist against her heart and flashed the imaginary Timmy a peace sign.

Mr. Halloway just sighed. "Raven . . ."

Raven shook her head and tried to look modest. "I know what you're going to say, Mr. Halloway. But really and truly, I'm no hero. Anyone would have sucked out that poison."

"Your bravery is an inspiration to us all," he said drily. "You're late. Now sit."

Raven hurried over to join Eddie and Chelsea at the lab table.

Eddie couldn't believe it. "Rae! *A snakebite?* That was worse than your quicksand excuse."

"I know," Raven agreed in a whisper. "I gotta work on those. But you're never going to believe what happened in the hall."

Chelsea leaned over with a worried frown. "I know. We're really going to have to do something about that snake problem."

Eddie exchanged a look with Raven. Man! he thought. Good thing for Chelsea she had the two of them for friends. She was so dense it worried him sometimes.

"No, Chelsea," Raven said. "I'm going to the Blue Rain concert with Devon."

Eddie felt his eyebrows shoot up. Wow! A date for the Blue Rain concert! This thing with Raven and Devon looked like it might be shaping up to be serious.

"You are *not* going to that Blue Rain concert with Devon!" Mrs. Baxter announced that afternoon. Raven and her mother were in the kitchen, and Mrs. Baxter was setting the table for dinner.

"Why not?" Raven demanded. She couldn't

believe her mom wasn't totally excited. Didn't she get it? Couldn't she see?

Devon Carter, the most gorgeous guy in the world, wanted to take her, Raven Baxter, to a Blue Rain concert. Didn't her mom understand that this might be the most important date of Raven's life?

"I got a call from your science teacher, Mr. Halloway," Mrs. Baxter said. "He said that you've been totally distracted lately."

Raven stared into space, her mind still on Devon. Maybe her mom didn't realize that in addition to being gorgeous and cool, he was a great dresser and one of the most popular boys at school. Raven looked down at her book cover. She had drawn a big DEVON on the front.

But the really great thing about Devon was that he wasn't popular in a jerky way. He was popular in a nice way. The way any mother would be proud to—

"*Raven!* Are you listening to me?" Mrs. Baxter demanded.

Oops! Raven realized she'd sort of lost the thread of the conversation. "I'm sorry, Mom. I was thinking about Devon."

Mrs. Baxter put down a pot of African violets with an irritated thunk and arranged her face in a now-hear-this expression. "Raven, you need to get your priorities straight. If you don't pass science, there isn't going to be a Devon."

Raven started to panic. As nice as Mrs. Baxter was, she could put some majorly bad mojo on a person when she was mad. "Mom, what are you going to do to him?"

"Not to him. To *you*," Mrs. Baxter said sternly. "No Devon. No concerts. No nothing unless you pass that science project."

Bummer! Raven hated it when her mom played hardball. It looked like Raven was going to have to work hard to turn this thing around. In the meantime, she didn't want any static on the Devon connection. She reached for the phone. "Okay, well, I have to call Devon . . ."

Mrs. Baxter's eyes widened.

". . . and tell him I've got to get my priorities straight," Raven explained quickly.

She didn't want any static on the Mom connection either.

Chapter Two

Cory Baxter and his friend William stood in the living room, watching Mr. Baxter feed paper into the shredder.

ZZZZZZZZZZZZZZZZZZ went the shredder.

The paper turned into narrow strips of confetti and fell into the plastic see-through wastebasket attached to the shredding apparatus.

Mr. Baxter gave them a huge grin. "How cool is that?" He was as happy as a kid with a new toy. He eagerly fed another piece of paper into the shredder.

Frankly, Cory didn't get the attraction. "Dad! A shredder? Can't you just toss your junk in the trash?"

"You're taking a rather simple process and

overcomplicating it," William commented.

William was a little guy with a big brain. When he said stuff, it sounded a lot smarter than when Cory said it. But Cory liked him anyway.

"No, no, no," Mr. Baxter argued. "Look, we shred for many reasons. We shred for safety. We shred for security. But most of all, we shred because it's really, really fun!" He grabbed a handful of confetti strips out of the wastebasket. He held them over his bald head like a wig and spoke in a Jamaican accent. "Hey, mon, I got my shredlocks on, mon."

Cory groaned at the bad pun. But his dad was having too much fun to notice.

Mr. Baxter picked up the shredder's wastebasket and beat it like a drum. *"You put the paper in the shredder,"* he sang in a reggae rhythm. *"Ya, ya, ya. And you shred it, you shred it, you shred it all up."*

Cory began pelting Raven with grapes.

"Oh, look at our babies," Mrs. Baxter said.
"All dressed up and heading for the door."

"Sorry, we forgot our key," Chelsea said.

**"That's okay," Raven said.
"My chin broke the fall."**

Squish!

"Gotcha, Mr. B!" Eddie cried.
"Psyched your mind."

"Oh, trust me," Cory said. "She cares."

"She's still smilin'," Eddie said to Chelsea. "She must have had fun with Devon."

"Blue Rain!" Raven cried. "That's amazing!"

"Raven! Are you listening to me?"
Mrs. Baxter demanded.

"...You'd better think of something,"
Chelsea advised Raven.

"Rae, what kind of project is this?" Eddie said,
shaking his head. "It looks like garbage."

"Are you trying to make me think?"
Cory asked his mom.

Yes! Yes! Raven thought. There it is.
The missing piece. "I did it!" she cried.

"Is it on now?" Chelsea asked. "Okay. Wait, wait, wait. How about now?"

"Devon, what are you doing down there?" Raven called.

Mr. Baxter danced out the door with his head and shoulders twitching to his own reggae beat.

Cory was getting worried about his dad. He needed a hobby. Golf. Stamp collecting. Decoupage, maybe. Anything besides shredding. It was becoming an obsession with him.

Just then the doorbell rang.

Cory forgot about the shredder and turned to William. "William, that's Madison from school. She asked *me* to borrow a video game."

William looked puzzled. "Is that significant?" he asked.

Is that significant? This was the problem with little smart guys, Cory said to himself. They were so busy looking at the big picture, they forgot to focus on the details. They lost touch with the things that were important to the average fourth grader. "Yeah," Cory said. "She eats at the cool kids' table."

William looked startled. "Aren't we cool kids?"

"We're about this close," Cory explained, holding his fingers a few centimeters apart. "If we get in good with her, she'll take us over the top. But first I gotta answer the door."

Cory pulled open the front door and tried to look cool. It wasn't easy with a player like Madison standing less than two feet away. The girl was major big-time cool. You could just tell. Her hair, her clothes, her snotty look.

"Hey, Madison," Cory said. "Come in."

Madison looked at William and sneered. "What's up, Captain Brainy Pants?"

William didn't have a mean bone in his body. And he almost never minded when people teased him—probably because he didn't even realize people were teasing him. "I prefer to be addressed as William," he told her. "Interesting tidbit: I'm named after my great-great-uncle, a four-time chess champion who—"

Cory watched Madison's face. She was looking at William as if he were some kind of alien species. Cory spoke up to cut William off. "Okay, here's that game you wanted."

"Thanks." Madison took the game, but her eyes were still on William. She reminded Cory of a cat stalking a mouse. First she'd tease him a little, then she'd kill him.

"You want to stay and play it? Or we could go outside and hang," Cory said to Madison, desperate to divert her attention.

"That sounds cool," she agreed.

"If we're heading outside, I'll have to change into my play clothes," said William.

Arrgh! Bad move. Couldn't William sense the danger he was in? Cory wondered. Nobody over the age of two wore "play clothes." Cory decided to lighten things up. He would tease William into showing a little common sense.

"What's wrong with the clothes you're wear-ing?" he asked.

Another bad move. Madison circled William. "What's *not* wrong?" she sneered. "His pants are totally second-grade. And what's up with the shirt? Are those rubber duckies?" She pointed at the fabric and shot Cory a look of disbelief.

William nodded happily. "Don't they put a smile on your face?"

"Uh, no." Madison turned to Cory. "You know, on second thought, I . . . really have to be someplace."

"But you just got here!" Cory protested.

"Right. And now I have to go." Madison took the video game and walked out.

Cory stood there feeling embarrassed and angry. Why couldn't William just go with the flow? he thought. Take his cues from me? Why did he have to act like such a nerdy little know-it-all? He glared at William.

William gave him a puzzled look.

"Your shirt just cost us the cool table," Cory said angrily.

"Thanks for coming by, you guys. I wanted to run my project by you," Raven said.

Eddie and Chelsea were sitting on the bar stools in the Baxters' kitchen.

Raven had spent the last two days working on her science project. She really wanted to excel and show her parents that true love was not incompatible with good grades.

She pointed to her project with pride. "It's a papier-mâché volcano!" She grabbed a bottle of vinegar with a flourish. Once they saw her special effects, Chelsea and Eddie were going to freak!

Raven poured a small amount of vinegar into the top of the volcano. "Put your goggles on, y'all." She backed up and pretended to be frightened. "Watch out. It's gonna blow."

When the vinegar hit the baking soda, the papier-mâché volcano "erupted." Fake lava burbled up and leaked tamely down the sides.

Raven leaned to the left and then to the right, dodging imaginary igneous rocks. "Whoaaa! Look out!" she cried.

She waited for the applause.

Nothing.

Eddie rolled his eyes. "Rae, girl, you're spacing out. Didn't you hear Halloway say no volcanoes?"

No volcanoes! "When did he say that?" Raven asked.

"When you were saving Timmy from that snakebite," Chelsea reminded her.

Raven felt her good mood evaporate. "Well, I spent all my time on this. What am I supposed to do?"

Chelsea gave her a worried look. "I don't

know, Rae. But you'd better think of something. 'Cause if you don't, there's no Devon, no concert, no love, no future. You know, you'll end up a bitter old woman with her twenty-seven cats. So, good luck."

"Thanks!" Raven was *so* not grateful for Chelsea's sympathetic remarks. "Where am I going to get another project?" she asked desperately.

Just then Cory came into the room with his friend, William. Raven rolled her eyes. Cory and William had been having the same dumb argument for two days. Some stupid little-kid debate about what was cool and what wasn't.

"I'm sorry Madison doesn't think I dress cool," William was saying. "I don't win fashion contests, I win science fairs."

"Yo, Rae." Eddie pointed to William. "You should get Captain Brainy Pants over there to help you out."

"Please. The day I go to a little kid for help is . . ." Raven broke off. Suddenly, she had a mental picture of Devon's face. Love was not proud, she remembered. ". . . *today*," she announced.

"Do your thing, Rae," Eddie urged.

Chelsea nodded her head. "Oh yeah! 'Cause remember, Rae. Twenty-seven cats. Meow."

Eddie and Chelsea waved good-bye and left through the kitchen door.

Raven gave William her million-dollar smile. "William, my little scientific genius. Hey, since you're needing some help in the fashion area, and I may possibly need some help with a science project, maybe you and I can make a deal."

Cory stepped between them. "My client and I are listening."

"Okay, well, I can give your boy a cool

makeover, with an outfit designed by *moi*—if he whips me up a project that'll help me pass science."

It was a good deal. Cory knew it, and William knew it. The two boys looked at each other and nodded.

William stuck out his hand and Raven took it. They exchanged a firm handshake.

Cory put his arms around both of them, looking like a happy negotiator.

Chapter Three

William wasn't called Captain Brainy Pants for nothing. The next day Raven sat in the kitchen watching William demonstrate his . . . wait, make that *her* killer science project.

He had chemicals, test tubes, beakers, and bottles. Raven was lovin' it already. It looked *so* scientific!

William adjusted his safety goggles and combined some chemicals. Raven and Cory watched. "So, by mixing these chemicals in exact proportions in the proper order," William said, "we can change the molecular structure of this compound to produce . . ." He gave the test tube a little swirl. ". . . your science project."

Whoa! Raven's mouth fell open. Rising out

of William's test tube was the most incredible cloud of color she'd ever seen. It was beautiful, like magic. "That is so cool. It's like a rainbow in a bottle. How'd you do that?" she asked.

William smiled and held up a sheet of paper. "It's all in the formula!" he exclaimed.

Raven reached out to grab the paper, but Cory snatched it before she could get her hands on it.

"Uh, uh, uh. We had a deal," Cory reminded her. "It's time for my man's cool-over."

"His what? Oh, the outfit, right . . . I got you," Raven said.

Oh, no! Raven had spent most of the night before trying on her own clothes, trying to decide what to wear to the Blue Rain concert. She'd completely forgotten about coming up with a cool outfit for William.

Her eyes darted around the kitchen while she stalled for time. She spotted something on the kitchen table. Aha! "Come here, William," Raven said finally. "I'm about to hook you up right quick."

Raven grabbed a napkin off the kitchen table and tied it over William's head. "Here you go. Look! All the cool kids are wearing these. It's a do-rag."

Actually, it looked more like a babushka, but Raven hoped Cory and William wouldn't know the difference.

"It's a dishrag!" Cory complained.

It was no use. She was busted. Raven threw up her hands. "Okay, look, I had the design in my head. I sat down at the sewing machine, and then, Devon called and he wanted me to listen to this Blue Rain song. . . ." Her voice trailed off.

Just thinking about the conversation gave her shivers. Her eyelids felt heavy. Her mouth hung open slightly. Something about that

Devon . . . something about that song . . . it just sent her off into sweet dreamland.

"William did his part," Cory said angrily. "And what were you doing? Drooling over Devon!"

Raven snapped to with a jolt. "No, I wasn't!"

But she was. Talk about embarrassing. Raven quickly wiped a spot of drool from the side of her mouth and tried to look dignified.

"The deal is off the table," Cory announced. He grabbed the sheet of paper with the formula and ran around the kitchen island.

Raven cut across the kitchen to head him off at the pass.

Cory spun around and went the other way. Raven chased him. Around and around they went. But he was too fast.

Next thing she knew, he'd disappeared into the living room with William behind him.

Oh no! Raven's ticket to the Blue Rain

concert was escaping. She couldn't let that happen. No! No! No!

She charged after the two boys. She had to catch them before they did anything drastic like . . .

Arrgh!

Raven skidded to a stop. Cory and William were standing over the shredder. Cory handed the paper to William. "Go ahead, William. You know what you gotta do."

"William, no!" Raven cried.

William lowered the paper over the waiting teeth of the shredder.

"One more step, and this formula's confetti," Cory threatened.

Raven chewed the inside of her cheek, thinking. I have to get my hands on that formula. But how? *How?* she wondered. Call their bluff, that's how. I'm made of tougher stuff than they are, right?

"You know what, William? Go ahead and shred it," Raven said. Her voice was brittle and mocking. Too bad she wasn't in some kind of movie. "You think that's gonna make you tough? You think that's gonna make you a man? Make you *cool*? Please."

She fixed him with a level gaze and raised one eyebrow.

"It's worth a shot," William answered cheerfully. And with that, he dropped the paper into the shredder.

GRRIINNNNDDDDD!!!

Raven dropped to her knees in horror. "Noooooooooo!"

"Rae, what kind of project is this?" Eddie said, shaking his head. "It looks like garbage."

Eddie and Chelsea were in Raven's room. She had placed a couple of frantic phone calls to summon them.

She needed help. No! Not just help. She needed a miracle.

There had been no way to figure out which strips of paper in the shredder's wastebasket were the strips of paper with the formula. Raven had emptied the wastebasket's entire contents onto the floor of her room. Somewhere in all that paper was the science project formula. Her ticket to the Blue Rain concert. Her ride through the tunnel of love.

But where?

They were going to have to go through every single strip and try to paste the formula back together. It was like a giant jigsaw puzzle. Raven sighed heavily.

"Eddie, come on, don't be a project-hater," Chelsea chirped. She gave Raven a grin of encouragement. It didn't help. Raven was beyond cheering up.

She swallowed hard, trying not to burst into

tears. "No. Y'all don't get it, okay. I messed up. William helped me, and I forgot to help him. So Cory got mad at me, and they shredded it. You know, the project's due tomorrow, and I really need you guys to help me tape the formula back together."

Eddie's eyes bugged out. "Rae, it's impossible!" he cried.

"Yeah. Maybe it is." Raven felt a big lump rise in her throat. What was the use? Her romance with Devon was over before it had even started.

Then suddenly, she felt herself spinning through the atmosphere. Eddie, Chelsea, and the huge pile of paper strips receded *way* into the back of her consciousness.

**Through her eye
The vision runs
Flash of future
Here it comes—**

I see myself in my own room. All the confetti is gone.

I see myself in my robe. I'm lying across my bed, looking at a book. I hear the music of Blue Rain in the background.

AND MY FACE IS BLUE!

ALL RIGHT!

Raven came skidding back to the present and hit the brakes. If her face was painted blue in the vision, she figured that *had* to mean she had been to the concert.

And if she'd heard the Blue Rain music, it was probably because Devon had given her the CD to play when she got home—so she could relive the most wonderful, romantic, and fabulous date of her life.

And the only way she could have gone on that date was if Mr. Halloway had given her parents the thumbs-up.

And the only way he would have given them the thumbs-up was if she had turned in a decent science project.

And the only way she would have turned in a decent science project was if she'd managed to find the formula and created that kick-butt rainbow in a beaker.

Raven noticed Eddie and Chelsea watching her. They knew about her premonitions, and they were waiting to hear what she had just seen.

"I had a vision," she announced. "My face was blue. I heard the Blue Rain music. I must have been at that concert with Devon. Which means the formula must have been taped back together."

Chelsea threw up her hands. "What? Hello? That means you passed your project. Yes!"

"Yes!" Raven shouted.

"Hey, congrats, Rae!" Eddie laughed.

"Yes, congrats. You did it, little missy," Chelsea cheered.

The nice thing about friends like Eddie and Chelsea? They were always happy for Raven when good things happened to her. Which was more than you could say for some members of her own family. Like, say, Cory.

"I did it!" Raven crowed. "I did it. Thank you, guys."

Chelsea opened her arms wide and hugged Raven. "I knew you could do it." Raven turned and hugged Eddie. Eddie gave Chelsea a big squeeze. Chelsea squeezed Eddie back and hugged Raven again before heading out the door.

Eddie gave her a way-to-go signal.

Raven was so moved. Those guys were just the best. "Aw, thank you. I'll see you at school tomorrow." She began to sing, serenading her friends as they thumped down the stairs to go home. "Yes. Whoo, yeah. I'm going to the concert."

Raven bobbed her head and twitched her shoulders, turning back to look at her room.

She was all set. Now, Raven thought, is there anything else I need to do—besides pick out a great outfit to impress Devon?

She started toward her closet and suddenly realized she was knee deep in confetti. "Oh, snap!" she wailed.

She'd gotten so excited over her vision, she'd completely forgotten the one teeny, tiny thing she had to do to make it a reality.

Find the formula!

Chapter Four

Meanwhile, downstairs, Cory was passing through the living room when the doorbell rang. His mom was reading on the sofa, so Cory hurried to open the door.

It was William. He was back. With a brand-new look.

After the shredding incident, he'd said he was going to work on his wardrobe issues himself.

William did a 360-degree turn, modeling his new outfit. "Greetings. What do you think? Totally duck free."

Cory could barely keep the irritation out of his voice. Did William really think this was a solution? High-waisted chinos! A polo shirt—

tucked in! "Man, take that shirt out of your pants. That's not cool." Cory grabbed the waist of William's shirt and gave it a hard tug.

Oops!

Two inches of plaid underwear appeared above the waistband of William's pants.

"My mom pinned my shirttail to my underwear," William explained.

Cory groaned. "You're killing me, man. Madison will be here any minute."

William's face fell. "Then I'll sneak out the side door to save you further embarrassment." He hung his head and hurried through the door leading to the kitchen.

Cory felt bad. But hey! What was a guy supposed to do?

Mrs. Baxter laid down her book. "What's happening, Cory?" she asked.

"He was tucked *and* pinned!" Cory plopped down on the couch next to his mom. Maybe just this once, his mom would remember what it was like to be a kid instead of a grown-up.

Grown-ups didn't care if they were cool or not. Which was a good thing, since they never were.

"Let me get this straight," said Mrs. Baxter. "You want to be friends with someone who makes fun of your best friend?"

"Yeah . . . uh . . . no . . . uh . . ." Cory looked at his mom. "Are you trying to make me think?"

Before Mrs. Baxter could answer, the doorbell rang again.

"Don't think too much—you've got a door to answer," she said.

Cory ran to the door. But he waited till his mom had walked into the kitchen before he opened it. He didn't want an audience.

As soon as the kitchen door closed behind Mrs. Baxter, he eagerly let Madison in.

"Hey, Cory. Cool shirt," she said.

Cory preened. "Hey, you know how I do," he said in his coolest voice.

"Where's Captain Brainy Pants?" Madison joked. "Oh, I forgot, it must be nap time."

Cory wished she would lay off William. "He's not a bad guy once you get to know him," Cory said defensively.

Madison looked skeptical. "What are you trying to say?" she asked.

Cory wished he'd kept his mouth shut. He didn't want to argue with Madison. He wanted to be her friend. To hang with her and her cool friends. "I don't know," he hedged. "I'm still thinking."

Madison made a little impatient sound and put her hands on her hips. "Listen, Cory, you could be cool. But if you stick up for him, that makes you a nerd, too."

Her body language was clear. *Do what I say—OR ELSE!*

Now she had gone too far. If anybody was going to push people around, make threats, and act like a general menace to society, Cory thought, it was going to be *him*.

Madison was a bully. And everybody knew the best way to deal with bullies was to stand up to them. "Okay. I'm done thinking. If being cool means dissing my friend, then I don't want to be cool."

"You were this close to sitting at our table," Madison sneered, holding up her fingers to indicate an inch.

Cory twisted his face into an equally nasty sneer. "And you are this close to the door. Let me show you out, nerd style." He swung his arm around and around and pointed to the exit.

"You're making a big mistake," Madison warned, walking out.

As far as Cory was concerned, he'd already

made it. His mistake was being mean to William. "Buh-bye, now." He closed the door with a slam.

Wow! That felt good, Cory thought. It wasn't every day you could be totally rude to somebody and feel that you'd done the right thing. Cory hurried over to the phone and punched in William's telephone number.

William picked it up on the first ring.

"William, it's Cory. I just wanted to say I'm sorry."

Cory took a deep breath. He owed his friend a big apology. A mega-apology. An apology with bells and whistles. And Cory was getting ready to deliver one.

Unfortunately, there was a knock on the door before he could get into his groove. Cory hurried to the door and opened it.

Amazing!

William was standing there, holding his

cell phone. "Apology accepted," William announced.

Cory grinned.

He'd never been so happy to see his friend.

Late that night—actually, early the next morning—Raven's eyelids felt like they were lined with sandpaper. Her eyeballs kept crossing. She'd been sorting and reading narrow spaghetti strips of paper for—she looked at the clock—thirteen hours. Raven swayed dizzily.

She'd sorted and sorted, looking for a piece here and a piece there. Little by little, the formula was actually falling into place.

The piece of paper with the formula was taped to her mirror. It was almost complete. Almost, but not quite. All she needed was one missing piece.

One vitally important missing piece.

Raven swayed again on her feet. She'd never felt this close to passing out in her life. She looked down at the strips of paper taped to her sweater, hoping to spot the one missing piece.

There were a couple of strips pasted to her chin with spit. She looked at one of them. The numbers blurred. She blinked, trying to clear her vision. Yes! Yes! she thought. There it is. The missing piece. "I did it!"

She leaned forward and pasted it up on the mirror. Oh, man! she said to herself. That William is a genius. She looked at the formula. Okay. It was complicated. No way could she memorize it.

But it was like a recipe. As long as she followed the directions—exactly—it would turn out just fine.

It had to. It was science!

"Time for bed," she muttered happily. She

collapsed on the bed and closed her eyes. Two and a half seconds later the alarm went off with a loud *BRRINNNNNG!* "Time for school," Raven corrected, pushing herself up off the bed with a groan.

Chapter Five

Half an hour later, Raven sat down in the kitchen to eat a bowl of cereal. The rumpled taped-up paper was on the counter beside her.

Maybe if she put her head down on the table and let her mind rest for two minutes, she could recharge her batteries. She put her head down. Immediately, she began to drift off and dream.

She dreamed she was sitting in the kitchen, taking a short nap. In her dream, she was happy because she knew she had her science project in the bag. Well, it wasn't actually in the bag, it was on the counter.

She dreamed her dad came in the kitchen,

carrying his shredder and singing his reggae shredder song.

"*You put the paper in the shredder and you shred it, you shred it, you shred it, you shred it all up now. Put the paper in the shredder . . .*"

In her dream, not even her dad's shredder fixation and his stupid shredder song could bother her because she was *so* happy about her science project.

"Hey, Rae," said Mr. Baxter. "Did you fall asleep down here?"

"Yeah," Raven muttered, figuring she was talking in her sleep.

"Well, you'd better get going to school," he told her.

"Yeah," Raven agreed. In her dream, she got up and headed for the door.

"And don't forget your lunch. Is tuna okay?" he asked.

"Yeah." In her dream, Raven reached out and

grabbed the paper sack with her lunch in it. Just then Mr. Baxter picked up a piece of paper lying on the counter. "Is this trash?"

"Yeah," Raven murmured.

In her dream Mr. Baxter began singing again.

"You put the paper in the shredder and you shred it, you shred it, you shred it, you shred it all up now. Put the paper in the shredder . . ."

ZZZZZZZZZZZZZZZZZZZZZZZZZZZ ZZZZZZZZZZZZZ.

A hideous grinding noise woke Raven up.

As soon as she woke up, she realized she had never been asleep. But she was still having a nightmare.

Mr. Baxter was standing right there. And he was shredding her formula!

"No! No!" she screamed. "You just shredded my science project!"

Mr. Baxter looked alarmed. "You said it was trash!"

Raven was almost hysterical. "It took me all night to put it together. Now it's no Devon. No concert. It's just gonna be me and twenty-seven cats." Raven fell to her knees and held her head in her hands.

Mr. Baxter was almost as upset as Raven. "Okay, look, look, look, look, look. I'll fix it, okay? Daddy'll fix it. So you just go to school, and I'll bring it to you, okay?"

Raven lifted her head. "Really?" she asked hopefully.

"Yeah," he said in a serious voice. "And then I'm going to get help for my shredding problem."

Raven smiled at her dad. He was so great. Having him for her dad almost made up for having Cory as a brother, she thought to herself. She gave him a kiss and rushed out the door.

Behind her, Mr. Baxter began unwinding a huge ball of shredded paper.

* * *

Later that morning, Eddie stood at the front of the class with two basketballs, an air pump, and a height chart. "So the amount of air pressure in a basketball is directly proportional to the height of the bounce. See?"

Raven checked her watch for about the tenth time. Science class was half over, and Mr. Baxter still hadn't shown up with the formula.

"Good, good," said Mr. Halloway. "Well researched, Eddie."

"*And* I can do this." Eddie flipped up the basketball and let it spin on the tip of his finger.

"Don't push it." Mr. Halloway grinned and motioned for Eddie to sit down.

Eddie sat.

Mr. Halloway's eyes swept the room. "Well, we've had some very interesting projects so far.

Especially Chelsea's attempt to convert brain waves into electricity."

Raven looked over at Chelsea. Sometimes Raven really worried about the girl.

Chelsea sat up proudly. She was still wearing the helmet from her science project. She looked like she was concentrating hard enough to pull a muscle. She glanced upward, trying to see the lightbulb on the top of her helmet. "Is it on now? Okay. Wait, wait, wait. How about now?"

Somehow Mr. Halloway managed to keep a straight face. "We'll get back to you, Chelsea. And now, at last, we'll hear from Raven Baxter."

"Chelsea, my dad's not here with the formula yet," whispered Raven.

Chelsea took a break from trying to light up her helmet. "*What?* You have to stall." The light on Chelsea's helmet flickered. "Ooh, it worked," Chelsea said happily. "I had a thought."

While the class focused its attention on Chelsea's flickering light, Raven slid out of her seat. She reluctantly walked to the front of the room.

Stall, huh? Raven thought. Shouldn't be too hard. She'd been doing it all year.

The lab table up front was covered with beakers full of liquid, bottles full of chemicals, and a variety of powders. She had no idea what any of them were.

The class fell silent. All eyes were on her. They were waiting.

Stall . . . stall . . . stall. Raven smiled as widely as she could. If I take my time with the intro, she thought, maybe my dad will get here in time. "Mr. Halloway, classmates, friends. What's up? How ya doing?"

"You're not running for president," Mr.

Halloway reminded her. "Just get to the project."

"Getting to the project! Yes, this is the plan. To the project we must get. Let's see . . . I'll need these." She reached for some glass swizzle sticks. "You know what? Before we start with that project, which we are getting to, I've got a crazy chemistry joke for Mr. Halloway. What did the beaker say to the test tube?"

"You're getting an F," he said.

Raven pretended she thought he was kidding. "You've heard this one before. Don't ruin it for the people. No, really. That's cool. But seriously, people, all right. Let's get it. Crank it up in here."

She was babbling. But she couldn't stop herself. Maybe it was lack of sleep or something.

Raven tapped a beaker with the glass swizzle stick. It played a musical note. Raven tapped a couple of other beakers and played a little riff. "Oooh. Give me a beat, Eddie!" she cried.

Eddie began drumming on his notebook cover.

Raven whaled on the beakers and started to dance.

Chelsea picked up the beat, banging on the lab table.

Oh yeah! This was some first-class stalling.

The beat was good. The class was into it. Raven swiveled her hips and shoulders, drumming on everything within reach.

She needed a dance partner. She spotted the anatomy skeleton. He was a little skinny, she thought, but he'd do.

Raven grabbed the skeleton and stomped down the center of the classroom. She drummed her glass swizzle sticks on the skeleton's ribs. Hmm, she wondered. Could I figure out some scientific explanation for why tapping on the top rib sounded slightly different from tapping on the bottom?

Mr. Halloway did not look entertained. He signaled Raven and the rest of the class to be quiet. "Raven! At what point do you plan to . . ." He glanced at the list of student projects. ". . . alter the chemical properties of a given solution, thereby producing the complete spectrum of primary colors?"

"Raven's gonna do what?" Raven smiled weakly. "Oh, Mr. Halloway, you're talking about 'Rainbow in a Bottle.' I'm getting to that. This is just a warm-up."

She went back to the lab table up front and tried to look confident. "Maybe I'll get lucky," she muttered. She looked at the beakers, powders, and bottles. "All right. A dash of this." She sprinkled some yellow powder into a beaker full of liquid that smelled sort of like ammonia. "Let's hook it up."

What else? She spotted a little bottle of

brownish liquid. "Ooh. Devon has a shirt this color." She added the entire bottle.

The contents of the beaker bubbled gently. Okay. Okay. Something was happening.

Little bottles of green liquid were lined up side by side. "Ooh. These are pretty." Into the brew they went. Ditto a pinch of pink powder. "A pinch of this. A dash of this." Raven smiled at her audience, hoping to inspire confidence. "Bam!" she joked, hurling some blue pellets into the mix like a TV chef.

Her concoction bubbled and smoked. "We're getting something, people. Clearly, we are getting something." Raven couldn't believe it. She was actually producing a chemical reaction. "It looks like science, people. You guys, it looks so scientifical."

She peered down into the beaker. The solution started to turn blue. Sort of an angry blue. Little puffs of blue steam spurted upward.

Now she was nervous. "Okay, you can stop now. Stop! Un-bam!" she ordered.

Glub! Blub! Burp!

Blue foam rose up out of the beaker and spilled over the sides. Raven tried to contain the foam, putting her hands over the top.

No use. It really was a volcano. Foamy blue lava spilled off the table and spread across the floor.

Now Mr. Halloway was alarmed. "Raven!" he cried. "You've produced an unstable chemical reaction!"

That sounded pretty impressive. "That's got to be worth, like, what, a C?"

A blue bubble rose to the top of the beaker and started to inflate.

"Everybody out!" Mr. Halloway shouted. "That thing's gonna blow. Come on. Everybody out! Quickly! Quickly!"

Eddie, Chelsea, and the whole class jumped

up and ran for the door. Mr. Halloway signaled to Raven to get out.

The blue bubble was now the size of Raven's head. She ran for the door. Then she ran back to her lab table. "Forgot my tuna."

She grabbed her lunch sack just as her dad came running in.

He was waving a piece of paper. "Here I am, baby. I've got your formula! Where is everybody?" He noticed the big blue bubble and smiled. "Ooh, cool!"

Raven pulled on his sleeve. "Uh, Dad, maybe we should—"

KABOOM!

The bubble exploded and sent a spray of blue mist in every direction.

"Oh, snap!" Raven groaned as the whole world—turned blue.

Chapter Six

Raven stared at her face in the bedroom mirror. Talk about a case of the blues! She'd washed her face for almost an hour, but it was still blue. "Girl," she said to her reflection, "you are so ready for that Blue Rain concert."

"So am I." A face appeared behind her in the mirror. Her dad! His face was as blue as hers.

Raven turned around and saw her mother too. "You know you're not going anywhere for a long time," Mrs. Baxter said firmly.

"Yeah, I know," Mr. Baxter said unhappily.

Mrs. Baxter rolled her eyes. "I'm talking to *Raven.*"

"Mr. Halloway said this blue's not going to

fade for another two days," said Mr. Baxter.

Mrs. Baxter grimaced. "I hope you learned your lesson," she said to Raven.

Raven's shoulders slumped. "Yeah, don't go back for the tuna."

Mr. and Mrs. Baxter looked even less amused by her humor than Mr. Halloway.

Okay. Raven knew she had to step up to the plate and take responsibility for her actions. Time to show some maturity. "I was so caught up in having a boyfriend, I forgot about everything else. And I'm really, really sorry."

"And what about William doing your science project?" Mr. Baxter prompted.

"That was wrong, too," Raven admitted. "Again, I am so, so sorry." She sneaked a peek at Mrs. Baxter's face. Was any of this having an effect? she wondered. But she couldn't tell.

"Am I ever gonna see Devon again?" Raven asked in a small voice.

"Well, when you get off punishment and make up your science project and do your extra credit for Mr. Halloway, then we'll talk about it," Mrs. Baxter answered in a stern voice.

Raven knew better than to push it. She nodded and turned back toward the mirror.

As her parents left the room, she heard her mom ask, "Victor, how are you feeling?"

"Kinda blue," he joked.

You and me both, Raven thought gloomily. She plopped down on her bed and opened her science textbook. "I guess I'd better get started."

She stared at the science textbook. A lump rose in her throat, and tears stung her eyes. "Oh, snap!" she choked. She had made a total fool out of herself. Devon probably never wanted to see her again anyway.

Raven fiercely wiped the tears away and

tried again to focus on her science book. Somewhere outside, somebody was playing music. It was a Blue Rain song. Wow! she thought. Talk about ironic.

Her shoulders swayed to the music as she turned the page.

Then suddenly, she realized what was happening.

"Just like in my vision!" she cried. She jumped up and ran over to the window to see if she could figure out where the music was coming from.

Underneath the window was Devon. His face was painted blue, and he held a boom box over his head. The Blue Rain music was coming from his boom box.

Raven's heart began to hammer. "Devon, what are you doing down there?" she asked.

"I figured if you couldn't go to the concert, then I'd bring the concert to you," he replied.

Raven was thrilled. Devon did want to see her. He cared. He really cared.

That meant she was going to have to buckle down and show him she cared, too. "Devon, I love that you did that . . . but if I'm ever gonna see you again, I have to get to work, okay?"

He smiled and nodded.

Raven shut the window. Was Devon an understanding guy or what? Raven couldn't believe how lucky she was.

"Just one more look," she promised herself. She opened the window, looked down at Devon, and sighed. Then she closed it and went over to the bed, where her homework was spread out.

Back to the world of science. Oh, the things we do for love, she thought, picking up her notebook.

* * *

"Well, everybody, I finished my project," Raven announced a few days later.

Her family was sitting on the couch, watching TV. Mr. Baxter clicked it off. His face was back to normal, and so was Raven's. "Rae, I thought you turned in your science project already."

"Oh, I did! This is my other project." She threw back her head and shouted, "William, come on down! Come on, Big Willy."

William came down the stairs, and every Baxter face lit up. Raven had really outdone herself this time. She'd given William the works: cool hair, clothes, shades. All by Raven.

"William, check you out," said Mrs. Baxter with a smile.

William did a runway pivot. "Yes, check me out. Pop the collar." He turned up the collar of his jacket.

Cory stared at William. "You look . . . cool!" he crowed.

"Bam!" yelled Raven.

William unzipped his jacket to show them the lining. It was made out of his old rubber-duck shirt. Personal style was an essential ingredient in the formula for cool.

"What can I say?" Raven told her family. "The man loves his ducks. Work it out for the people."

Mr. and Mrs. Baxter applauded.

Cory gave William a high five, and the two of them began to boogie.

Raven watched happily, feeling that maybe she really had learned some lessons. Not just about science. About life.

The lesson? Do the right thing, she said to herself. 'Cause when you do the right thing, life is . . . a snap!

BAM!

Gaze into the future and take a sneak peek at the next *That's So Raven* story. . . .

Adapted by Kimberly Morris

Based on the television series, "That's So Raven", created by Michael Poryes and Susan Sherman

Based on the episode written by Michael Feldman

"*Miss you, wanna kiss you. Miss you, wanna kiss you. Miss you, wanna kiss you.*" Raven Baxter couldn't get the lyrics out of her head.

Not that she cared. After all, she was doing this for Devon.

Raven wrestled the six-foot by four-foot valentine "card" she had made down the stairs.

"Ugghhh," she grunted as she pulled the card down the last step and dragged it into the kitchen. She propped her creation against the wall and stood back to admire it.

Wow! It was amazing—probably the world's biggest valentine. It had to be the world's heaviest.

Her mom, dad, and brother, Cory, were at the table eating breakfast. "Morning," Raven chirped nonchalantly.

Mr. Baxter turned around to see what all the commotion was about. When he saw the huge red card with a lacy heart, he smiled. "Awwww. Valentine's Day is coming up, and Rae made Daddy a big ol' valentine's card."

"Sorry, Daddy, it's for Devon. Uh, he's visiting his grandma in L.A., and y'know, I just wanted to send him a little card to remind him of *moi*." Raven was actually glad her whole family was here. She had really outdone herself this time, and she was eager to show off her handiwork. Raven reached up and pulled on the front of the card. It swung open like a door.

Inside the giant card, a huge Raven head made from foam board swiveled back and forth, singing, *"Miss you, wanna kiss you. Miss you, wanna kiss you. Miss you, wanna kiss you."*

The only problem was that sometimes the voice chip got stuck.

"Miss you, wanna kiss you. Miss you, wanna kiss you. Miss you, wanna kiss you."

Cory grinned. "Uh, yeah, that'll remind him of you. A big ol' head that won't stop talking."

"Miss you, wanna kiss you. Miss you, wanna kiss you. Miss you, wanna kiss you."

Raven shot Cory a withering look. Then she

slammed the card shut to make it stop singing.

"So, how 'bout you, Cory? You got a Valentine?" asked Mrs. Baxter.

"Oh, yeah. A new girl in school." Cory's eyes grew dreamy. "Danielle," he said with a sigh.

"Oooh, that is beautiful, Cory. *Danielle.*" Raven repeated the name and pretended to muse. "I think that's French for 'Girlie, you better run before it's too late.'" She started to laugh at her own sarcastic joke. But suddenly, everything in the kitchen seemed to spin off into the distance.

Only her family and her two best friends knew it, but Raven Baxter was psychic. Sometimes, right out of nowhere, she would get a glimpse of the future. Not a big hunk of it or anything. Just a little snippet. But a lot of times it was more than enough to let her know when something major was about to go down.

Through her eye
The vision runs
Flash of future
Here it comes—

I see Cory. He's in our living room, wearing an athletic suit like the ones that rappers wear. Little pieces of confetti are falling all around him—he looks heartbroken. "Nobody wants to be my valentine," he says sadly. Ohmigosh, he's actually crying! Poor little guy.

Raven snapped back into the present. Oh man! Her little brother was about to get run over in the tunnel of love.

Sure, he was a horrible, obnoxious toad. But still, she was his sister. And there was nothing worse than crying on Valentine's Day.

"Cory, have you actually talked to Danielle yet?" she asked.

"No. I've been waiting to make my move. And today is moving day." Cory said suavely.

"Listen, this may sound weird, but I want you to have a good Valentine's Day, Cory, okay?" Raven said kindly.

Cory's eyes narrowed with suspicion. "Why?"

"Because I know a little somethin', somethin' about romance, and I wanna help a brother out."

Mr. and Mrs. Baxter looked even more suspicious than Cory. "Why?" they asked in unison. Raven and Cory never tried to help each other out.

But Raven was actually sincere this time. "Listen, all I'm saying is when you talk to Danielle, don't mess up. Think about what you're gonna say before you say it."

Cory rolled his eyes, like he couldn't believe she was actually trying to give *him*—Mr.

Cool—advice. "Don't worry about me. I know how to talk to the ladies."

Now Raven was even more worried. She knew that sometimes it was better to *listen* to the ladies. And Cory wasn't exactly what you'd call a good listener.

Later that morning, Cory watched Danielle across the classroom. Wow! She was even cuter than he remembered. He loved the way she did her hair in three ponytails.

Danielle saw Cory and smiled. "Oh, hi, Cory."

Cory opened his mouth to say something cool to impress her, but suddenly, his tongue seemed stuck to the roof of his mouth. "Hum-a-na, hum-a-na, hum-a-na," he said.

Cory swallowed. What was wrong? He was usually such a smooth talker. "Hum-a-na, hum-a-na, hum-a-na," he repeated.

Danielle gave him a skeptical smile, as if she wasn't sure if he was genuinely tongue-tied, or if he was making fun of her. "Okay. Nice talking to you." She picked up her books and walked away.

Cory felt like kicking himself. No, not himself. "Raven," he said in disgust. She'd psyched him out! That whole being-a-nice-sister act was all part of her evil plan. And he had actually fallen for it.

A COMEDY OF PSYCHIC PROPORTIONS!

that's SO raven

EVERY DAY ON DISNEY CHANNEL!

The new book series.
Available wherever books are sold.

W.i.t.c.h.

Will   Irma   Taranee   Cornelia   Hay Lin

The magic of friendship

Collect them all!

Make some powerful friends at www.clubwitch.com

Betty and Veronica wear the latest fashions, know what's cool, and are always up for some fun. Now they are telling all to their fans! Full of humor and attitude, these books will show you how to deal with everything from school to boys—all from the perspective of two famous and fabulous best friends . . . and crush rivals!

Available wherever books are sold!

For more fun with Archie and the gang, log onto www.archiecomics.com.

HYPERION
BOOKS FOR CHILDREN
miramax books